OCT -- 2004

Guess Who?

Written by Diane Namm

Illustrated by David Sheldon

My First
READER

children's press ®

A Division of Scholastic Inc.
New York Toronto London Auckland Sydney
Mexico City New Delhi Hong Kong
Danbury, Connecticut

Library of Congress Cataloging-in-Publication Data

Namm, Diane.
  Guess who? / written by Diane Namm ; illustrated by David
Sheldon.
       p. cm. – (My first reader)
Summary: Inspired by toys and other objects in his room, a boy
imagines all sorts of visitors, from a jet pilot to slimy aliens, as
he thinks about who might come and play with him.
  ISBN 0-516-24412-4 (lib. bdg.)   0-516-25503-7 (pbk.)
  [1. Imagination–Fiction. 2. Play–Fiction. 3. Stories in rhyme.] I. Sheldon,
David, 1957- ill. II. Title. III. Series.
  PZ8.3.N27Gu 2004
  [E]–dc22
                                    2003014072

Text © 2004 Nancy Hall, Inc.
Illustrations © 2004 David Sheldon
All rights reserved.
Published in 2004 by Children's Press, an imprint of Scholastic Library Publishing.
Published simultaneously in Canada.
Printed in the United States of America.

1 2 3 4 5 6 7 8 9 10 R 13 12 11 10 09 08 07 06 05 04

Note to Parents and Teachers

Once a reader can recognize and identify the 30 words
used to tell this story, he or she will be able to successfully
read the entire book. These 30 words are repeated throughout
the story, so that young readers will be able to recognize
the words easily and understand their meaning.

The 30 words used in this book are:

a	girl	small
and	green	snake
bake	is	someone
ball	it	today
be	jet	twirl
big	me	visit
boy	or	who
can	pet	will
climb	play	with
come	slime	you

4

Who will visit me today?

Who will visit me and play?

Is it someone with a ball?

Is it someone big or small?

11

Is it someone with a pet?

Is it someone with a jet?

Is it someone with green slime?

Is it someone who can climb?

Is it someone with a snake?

Is it someone who can bake?

Is it someone who can twirl?

Will it be a boy or girl?

Who will visit me today?

YOU will visit! Come and play!

ABOUT THE AUTHOR

Diane Namm is the author of more than twenty-five books for children and young adults. Formerly an editor in New York, Namm freelances for a children's entertainment production company, writes, and lives in Malibu, California, with her husband and two children. Whenever company was coming when Namm was a little girl, she always hoped whoever it was would be someone fun. Sometimes it was, sometimes it wasn't. The visitors she liked the best would read with her and make her laugh, just like the little boy in this book.

ABOUT THE ILLUSTRATOR

David Sheldon has illustrated several books for children. He uses watercolors and acrylics on watercolor paper to make his images. Sheldon currently lives in Brooklyn, New York, with his wife, Margit, and their three children, William, Sarah, and Christopher. The Sheldon kids love to have different friends come and visit but, as far as they know, no aliens have shown up yet!